This Book Belongs to :

All the neighbors knew that, once again, the Farmer had turned a simple pumpkin into a simply glorious sight.

In the same way, God the Father offers His children the chance to be made new, full of joy and full of light, shining like stars in a dark world.

"If anyone belongs to Christ, then he is made new.
The old things have gone; everything is made new!" 2 Corinthians 5:17

The Pumpkin Patch Parable

by

Liz Curtis Higgs

Illustrated by Nancy Munger

Tommy
NELSON®

Thomas Nelson, Inc.
Nashville

Published in Nashville, Tennessee, by Thomas Nelson, Inc., Publishers, and distributed in Canada by Word Communications, Ltd., Richmond, British Columbia, and in the United Kingdom by Word (UK), Ltd., Milton Keynes, England.

Scripture quotations are from the International Children's Bible, New Century Version, copyright © 1986 by Sweet Publishing, Fort Worth, Texas 76137. Used by permission.

To contact the author, please write her :   Liz Curtis Higgs
                                                   P.O. Box 43577
                                                   Louisville, KY 40253-0577

Library of Congress Cataloging-in-Publication Data

Higgs, Liz Curtis.
        The pumpkin patch parable / by Liz Curtis Higgs ;
illustrated by Nancy Munger.
                p. cm.
        Summary: Tells a parable in which the farmer turns a simple pumpkin into a
glorious sight to illustrate that God wants His children to be full of light.
        ISBN 0-7852-7722-6
        1. Salvation--Juvenile literature. 2. Parables. 3. Christian life--Juvenile literature.
4. Halloween--Juvenile literature. [1. Parables. 2. Christian life.] I. Munger, Nancy,
ill. II. Title.
        BT751.2.H53 1995
        242'.62--dc20

                                                                                    95-8000
                                                                                       CIP
                                                                                        AC

                                        Printed in the United States

                                          11 12 13 14 - 01

A Note to Parents from the Author:

This book is NOT a celebration of Halloween . . . no ghosts, goblins, demons, witches, or monsters here!

As the mother of two young children, I wanted to offer an alternative message for our kids each autumn, something wholesome, positive and encouraging. Since the Lord Himself created pumpkins, it seemed appropriate to redeem this familiar symbol of the harvest season for His good purpose.

My prayer is that through this simple pumpkin parable your own heart will be filled with the light of God's love and you, too, will "let yourself glow!"

For Matthew and Lillian,
my favorite little pumpkins

See that big red barn? And those rolling green fields? That's where the Farmer lives, w-a-a-a-y out in the country. It's so far out the streets don't even have stop signs.

Fresh Vegetables

The Farmer grows lots of different things
in those fields. He grows tall green corn
and big red tomatoes . . .

. . . long yellow squash and little green peas.
People eat that stuff for dinner.

"I am the true vine; my Father is the gardener."
John 15:1

The BEST vegetables the Farmer grows are PUMPKINS! They start out as flat, oval seeds, almost as big as raisins.

"The kingdom of heaven is like a man who planted good seed in his field." Matthew 13:24

One hot June day, soon after school let out, the Farmer planted pumpkin seeds, just like He did every Summer.

The seeds disappeared into the ground in nice neat rows and grew there in the dark, all through the Fourth of July.

"This is what the story means:
The seed is God's teaching." Luke 8:11

Early one morning, a tiny green shoot quietly poked its way out of the soil. Soon, a long, green vine stretched across the ground. From that vine, little buds sprouted into wide green leaves.

The leaves spread out flat to catch the August sun.

Someday, those little green buds would turn into big orange pumpkins!

But not yet. The patient Farmer waited. And waited.

"God is being patient with you. He does not want anyone to be lost. He wants everyone to change his heart and life."
2 Peter 3:9

The pumpkins began to grow. How different they looked!

Some were tall and lean.

Some were short
and round.

Some had lumps and bumps.

ALL of them were pumpkins!

"'My hand made all things. All things are here because I made them,' says the Lord."
Isaiah 66:2

October came at last.
The sky was bright blue and the air was cooler.
Every night it got dark earlier than it did the
night before. It was time for the Farmer to
harvest His pumpkin crop.

The Farmer's many workers
brought lots of ripe pumpkins
in from the fields.
Which one would He choose first?

*"Open your eyes. Look at the fields that are
ready for harvesting now." John 4:35*

The Farmer picked up one large pumpkin,
being v-e-r-y careful not to let it slip through
His hands. Pumpkins are tough on the outside,
but break into smithereens if you drop them!
He washed off all the dirt, holding on tight.

"Get up, be baptized, and wash your sins away." Acts 22:16

Next came the messy part.

Pumpkins are full of dozens of seeds and lots of slimy pulp. The Farmer had a special plan for His chosen pumpkin, so the seeds and the slime had to go.

"Create in me a pure heart, God."
Psalm 51:10

He slowly slid a large knife right into the center of the pumpkin.

The pumpkin didn't make a sound, because vegetables don't talk. If they did talk, the pumpkin might have said, "Ouch!"

"God's word is alive and working. It is sharper than a sword sharpened on both sides. It cuts all the way into us . . . And God's word judges the thoughts and feelings in our hearts."
Hebrews 4:12

Gently, the Farmer
cut a round hole
in the top of the
pumpkin and
pulled on the stem.

Squishy,
stringy
pulp
waited for Him
inside . . . YUCK!

"I am the Lord, and I can look into a person's heart." Jeremiah 17:10

The Farmer pulled out all that slimy pulp, and wrapped it up in an old newspaper. Off to the compost pile it went, never to be seen again.

"He has taken our sins away from us as far as the east is from west."
Psalm 103:12

Then, something REALLY exciting happened:
The pumpkin got a new face!

"We all show the Lord's glory,
and we are being changed to be like him."
2 Corinthians 3:18

The Farmer
carved a
triangle
for
each
eye.

Pumpkins
have eyes
that don't
blink or
turn away.
They see
everything!

He neatly carved

a little square
for a nose,

and then a big,
w-i-d-e smile.

What happened next was wonderful.
The Farmer put a small, white candle down
inside the pumpkin and touched the wick with a
flame.

How that pumpkin glowed!

"God once said, 'Let the light shine out of the darkness!'
And this is the same God who made his light shine in our hearts."
2 Corinthians 4:6

As the sky grew darker, the pumpkin on the porch was shining brighter than ever.

When people saw the smiling pumpkin, they smiled back!

"In the same way, you should be a light for other people.
Live so that they will see the good things you do.
Live so that they will praise your Father in heaven." Matthew 5:16